A House for Lily Mouse

Michelle Cartlidge

Prentice-Hall Books for Young Readers
A Division of Simon & Schuster, Inc.
New York

Lily Mouse is leaving her home. All her family have been
caught in mousetraps and it is not safe to stay.

She sets off sadly into the country to find a new home.

First she comes upon an old boot by the side of the
road. It has holes in it and no laces, but Lily doesn't
mind.

"It's perfect for me," she says. "I've always wanted to
live in a nice, cosy old boot."

But just as she is about to go inside, out comes Mr.
Slithery Snail.

"Did you want something?" he asks.

"Oh, no, nothing at all," says Lily.

And she continues on her way.

A little farther on, Lily sees an old satchel.

"That would make a nice house for me," Lily thinks. "I can close it up when the weather is cold and open it when the sun shines."

But when Lily comes close, she finds it is already occupied, by a hedgehog with a very prickly nature.

"No visitors except by appointment!" he shouts.

"Sorry," says Lily, hurrying away.

No room in the boot, no room in the satchel....

What's this? A whole family of empty tins, all in good condition, with pretty colored labels.

Lily tries them all. But the sardine tin is really too small. The cream dessert tin is too sticky. The red beans tin is too slippery.

"I don't like these tins," Lily decides. "Anyway, you can't sing properly inside a tin — the echoes give you a headache." So poor Lily still hasn't found a house.

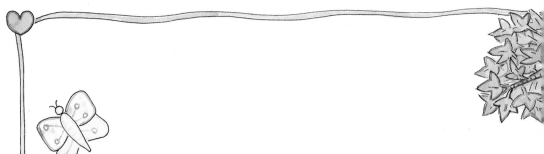

Then she sees something *wonderful*: a palace made of blue and white china. Its handle is missing and its spout is broken, but it is beautiful. A mouse queen could live there.

As Lily comes near, she sees smoke coming from the spout. And she can smell vegetable soup.

"Oh dear," sighs Lily.

The teapot lid lifts up, and a mouse pokes her head out.

"Hello," she says. "What's the matter?"

"Well," says Lily sadly, "I'm looking for a house and it's no good. Everything is taken."

"You could try a teacup," says the other mouse. "There are lots of them and some are quite whole."

And with that she pulls down the lid and goes back down into her teapot.

What a silly idea. Who could live in a teacup? It's just big enough to take a bath in before bedtime, and that is what Lily does. But where *can* Lily go to bed? She starts to cry.

"What shall I do? I've nowhere to go."

Along comes a sturdy fieldmouse, chewing wheat seeds.

"Hello, young mouse. What's wrong?"

Lily tells him all her sad story.

"I'm so unhappy! I can't find a house anywhere," she cries "I'll just have to sleep in a nasty, dirty ditch."

But Albert the fieldmouse laughs.

"You *are* silly," he says. "Look at your paws. Feel your teeth. What do you think they are for?"

"What do you mean?" asks Lily. "What about my paws and my teeth?"

"I'll show you." And Albert starts burrowing into the ground. With his paws and teeth he makes a hole and disappears down it.

"Where are you? What are you doing?" cries Lily.

"You'll see," calls Albert, as piles of earth are tossed out.

It's dark when she hears Albert's
voice calling, "Come down now."
What a surprise! He has dug a snug, roomy
underground home.
"It's lovely," says Lily. "But I've no furniture
— no belongings at all."

"That's easy," says Albert. "I'll help you make some furniture."

"Do you think I can?" asks Lily.

"Of course you can. A mouse can do anything when she puts her mind to it," says Albert.

And Lily finds she *can* make the furniture and paint it too, with a little help from Albert.

"Dear Lily, you are brave and clever and good at carpentry," says Albert. "Will you marry me?"

"Dear Albert," says Lily, "you make me feel brave and clever and good at carpentry. I *will* marry you."

And so Lily and Albert settle down in their cosy home. Not a boot, or a satchel, or a teapot, but a proper mousehouse, that is all their own work. And there they live happily for a long, long time.

Original French text © 1985 by Bayard Presse and Anne Marie Chapouton
Revised English text © 1986 by David Ross
Illustrations © 1986 by Michelle Cartlidge

Published by Prentice-Hall Books For Young Readers
A Division of Simon & Schuster, Inc.
Simon & Schuster Building
1230 Avenue of the Americas
New York, New York 10020
Published in Great Britain by Methuen Children's Books Ltd.
PRENTICE-HALL BOOKS FOR YOUNG READERS is a trademark of Simon & Schuster, Inc.

Printed in Singapore by Khai Wah Litho Pte Ltd

10 9 8 7 6 5 4 3 2 1